STOP Max!

Part of the Resilient Ratties Series

Giving children the skills to understand and manage their own emotions and mental health

Welcome to the Resilient Ratties Series! Follow Max and Lucy on their adventures whilst learning valuable life skills along the way.

I would like to take this opportunity to thank all of the amazing people that have helped to make this idea come to life!

Thank you

To my supportive husband Rikki and wonderful children Rian and Ellie, thank you for all your support and encouragement and listening to me talk about rats even more than usual!

Thank you to my wonderful family, friends and colleagues who have supported and encouraged me every step of the way, helping me to believe that this was possible.

A huge thank you to Carol and Michelle. The Decider Skills are truly life changing.

Thank you for all the work that you do and for giving me permission to share your work through the Resilient Ratties Series.

Thanks to Terry for his wonderful interpretations of my ideas and for bringing the Resilient Ratties to life!

And finally, Thank You to Fi and Becs from Fi and Books self-publishing.

Without your amazing 'Become an Author Competition', this would not have been possible.

Thank you for your encouragement, support, advice and professionalism within every page of this book.

Notes to adults

As a mental health practitioner for over 12 years, I have been supporting adults to learn skills in order to help manage and maintain their mental and physical well-being.

Through the Resilient Ratties series of children's books I hope to introduce both children and adults to a set of skills called **The Decider Life Skills**.

These skills have completely transformed not only my practice but also the lives of the individuals that I work with. Time and time again I hear people say "*I wish I had learned these skills years ago...*"

I hope you find these books both fun and educational. They have been written and designed to help you learn alongside your child in a way that they can understand, enjoy and remember.

You can use the '**Let's Learn Together**' section at the end of each book to open up conversations and encourage children to learn about how the skills apply to them and their surroundings, whether at home, school or playing outdoors.

The Decider
Winning strategies for mental health

About The Decider Life Skills

Giving children the skills to understand and manage their own emotions and mental health

The Decider Life Skills were developed in Guernsey by Michelle Ayres and Carol Vivyan, both CBT therapists with a background in mental health nursing. There are 12 individual skills aimed at tolerating distress, regulating emotions, increasing mindfulness and improving relationships. You can find out more information about The Decider Life Skills including training and delivery of the skills by visiting their website: **www.thedecider.org.uk**

Finally... why did I choose to bring the skills to life with my cartoon rats? I have four cheeky ratties of my own! Rats are incredibly misunderstood creatures but once you get to know them, they are extremely intelligent, adaptive and resilient characters who seek social connection and relationships! So why did I choose rats?... Why not!

me & ginger

ellie & alfie

the boys!
alfie, ralph, ginger & jinx

rian & ralph
(& jinx!)

First published in UK in 2020 by Fiona Woodhead from FiandBooks.com
67 The Hollins, Triangle, Halifax, West Yorkshire. HX6 3LU.
www.fiandbooks.com

www.fiandbooks.com

ISBN 978-1-909515-09-3

FI & BOOKS
BECOME-AN-AUTHOR
WINNER
2019

STOP Max!

Part of the Resilient Ratties Series

Giving children the skills to understand and manage their own emotions and mental health

Max woke bright and early. It was Saturday and Max was going to the park to see his friends. He couldn't wait to show them his new shiny helicopter.

But when Max got to the park things did not go to plan...

First of all, Max wanted to go on the slide, but it was too wet. Then Max tried to go on the swings, but every swing was being used! Next Max decided to go on the see-saw, but that was already taken too. He really wanted to play hide and seek with his friends, but he couldn't find them anywhere - he couldn't even show them his new shiny helicopter!

Max felt like he'd had enough, he could feel his heart beating faster and his face getting red. "It's not fair!" he shouted. "I don't like this anymore!" and he suddenly ran towards the road.

"STOP Max!" his mum shouted loudly. She pointed to the STOP sign and Max remembered the STOPP Skill that he had learned at school.

STOPP

S top and take a step back
T ake a deep breath
O bserve
P ull back and put in perspective
P ractice what works

Max stopped and stepped back from the road. He took one big, deep breath and started to feel calmer.

Max's mum asked him what he could observe inside his body. "Max, what is your Fizz right now?" she said. Max remembered his teacher Miss Boggle telling his class that our Fizz helps us to see what's happening inside our body when we feel angry, sad, happy or scared. Max could tell that he was on level 5 of his Fizz scale and he was feeling angry. He told his mum how his Fizz felt.

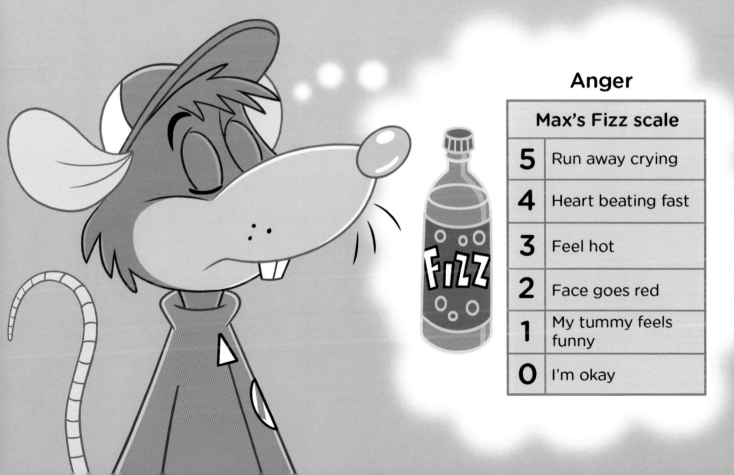

Anger

Max's Fizz scale	
5	Run away crying
4	Heart beating fast
3	Feel hot
2	Face goes red
1	My tummy feels funny
0	I'm okay

"That's great, Max well done!" his mum said with a smile on her face. "Now, can you pull back and see if you've missed anything that has happened?" Max looked down at the shiny yellow helicopter in his hand and he imagined flying high up in the sky and looking down below. By **pulling back and looking at the bigger picture,** Max could see things differently.

When he imagined the bigger picture Max could see his friends playing hide and seek in the park and he could also see lots of cars whizzing past on the busy road. He hadn't seen those cars before! He felt very glad that he hadn't run out onto the dangerous busy road.

Max told his mum that he was happy that he hadn't been hurt but he still felt angry that his friends didn't want to play with him. She knelt down and asked him kindly "Max, do you really think it's true that your friends don't want to play with you?"

Max's mum knew that sometimes looking at facts and talking about opinions can help us to think differently. At first Max didn't really understand what his mum meant. When he was angry, he found it hard to put his opinions into words. Max's mum patiently helped him to look at all the facts about being in the park and to see his own opinions.

FACT

✓ Max feels angry

✓ Max's friends are all playing and Max is not playing

✓ Max nearly ran on to the road

"I ran away because I was angry" Max said to his mum. Looking at the facts and understanding his opinions had helped him realise that he was angry because he couldn't find his friends. Not because they didn't want to play with him! Max's mum grinned. "Well done Max! So what's the best thing to **practise** to make you feel better?" she asked. Max sighed, smiled and replied. "I'd really like to play with my friends, can we go and find them?"

Max's mum took his hand and they walked back over to the park. He saw his friends playing hide and seek over in the bushes and ran over to say sorry for shouting and running away. Max's friends were excited to see him, and he proudly showed them his yellow helicopter, "Can I join in?" he asked. "Yes, of course Max!" they cheered and they all happily enjoyed their game of hide and seek.

Learning Together : The Fizz

When we feel different emotions like happy, sad, angry or scared,
we can sometimes feel different things happening inside our body.

In the story, Max was angry, and he could feel his heart beating faster and his face getting red. These feelings made him want to run away. This is called feeling the Fizz.

Anger

Max's Fizz scale	
5	Run away crying
4	Heart beating fast
3	Feel hot
2	Face goes red
1	My tummy feels funny
0	I'm okay

If we can learn to notice our Fizz, then we can do things to help lower our Fizz. Lowering your fizz might stop you from feeling even worse or doing things that could hurt you or hurt other people.

In the story, Max's Fizz was a level 5. This made him run away from the park and he nearly ran onto a busy road. He was so "fizzed-up" that he didn't even notice the dangerous cars whizzing past on the road.

Your Fizz Scale

What do you feel in your body when you are angry, sad, happy or scared?

Have a look at the Fizz bottle and see if you can describe your own Fizz.

You can ask an adult to help you! 0 = feeling okay and 5 = feeling fizzed-up.

Your Fizz scale	
5	
4	
3	
2	
1	
0	

Questions to ask and talk about together

Question 1: At the park, what happened to Max that made his Fizz go up?

Question 2: If Max had noticed his Fizz sooner, what could he have done differently instead of shouting and running away?

The STOPP Skill

The **STOPP** skill helps us to pause before reacting to something that has made us all fizzed up.

The different steps of the **STOPP** skill help us to notice **our Fizz** and think about what to do next.

S	Stop and take a step back
T	Take a deep breath
O	Observe
P	Pull back and put in perspective
P	Practice what works.

Questions to ask and talk about together

Question 1: What could have happened to Max if he didn't stop?

Question 2: Can you think of a time when using the STOPP skill could have helped you

Activity idea

Can you make your own **STOPP** sign to help you remember the skill?

The Fact or Opinion Skill

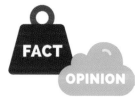

Sometimes looking at facts and talking about opinion can help us to think differently and check that what we are thinking is true.

In the story, Max's mum helped him to look at all the facts about being in the park and to see his own opinions.

By using the facts or opinions skill, Max realised that what he thought about his friends wasn't true.

Questions to ask and talk about together

Rat Fact
Rats chatter their teeth when they are stressed or happy, this is called bruxing

Question 1: What is a fact?

Question 2: What is an opinion?

Rat Fact
When rats are happy their eyes boggle (move in and out of their socket)

There is an App!

Further information about any of these skills can be found at **www.getselfhelp.co.uk**
You can also download the **STOPP App** for your mobile phone!

The Fact or Opinion Skill

You can practice the fact or opinion skill by using the table below...

Write down the thought you are having here:

What are the facts?	What are your opinions?
(a fact is something that has evidence to support it and cannot be argued with)	(an opinion is affected by emotion and will be different for different people)

Do you notice any changes to your thought now that you have looked at the **facts** and **opinions**?